An ANTY-WAR Story

(Ant)Tony Ross

Ⓐ

Andersen Press

At last, the ants found the perfect place

and so they built their Antworld on the spot.

The ants worked hard. Antworld was a happy place,
where lots of little ants were born.

One little ant was different: he had a name.
He did not know WHY he had a name, and neither
did the other ants. His name was Douglas.

Douglas watched the other ants form a beautiful
line. All day, they hurried past carrying food.
"Why do you do that?" asked Douglas.

"So we can eat it over here," was the reply.
"Why don't you eat it over there?" asked Douglas.
"Let's not talk about it!" was the reply.

Douglas thought that was a fine answer. Now he knew what he wanted to do with his life. He wanted to fit in, to carry food and be in the beautiful line.

But as he grew bigger, nobody asked Douglas to do anything at all. At last, he went to the Chief Ant. "I want to fit in," he said.

The Chief Ant examined his papers and his lists.
"Errrr… no!" he replied. "We have you down for
other things. Important things."

"You are a big ant. You have a big head, and big teeth." Douglas felt proud and very special. "We have you down as a soldier."

"I will gladly be a soldier," said Douglas.
"What is a soldier? Will I carry food and be
in the beautiful line?"

The Chief Ant waved his papers at Douglas.
"You will not carry food, you will carry a rifle."
Douglas felt sad. "But you will have a uniform."

Douglas was worried, but he promised he would do
his best. "What must a soldier do?" he asked.
"He must defend Antworld," replied the Chief Ant.

So Douglas proudly put on his uniform, glad that
his big head and big teeth would make Antworld
a safer place for the little ants.

With his rifle on his shoulder, Douglas joined
the beautiful line of soldiers as they marched
up and down and the little ants waved flags.

The band played and Douglas felt happy to be a
soldier, and to be in a beautiful line, and to
keep the little ants safe...

The end.

This book belongs to:

_ _ _ _ _ _ _ _ _ _ _

To Cliff, Nigel, Arlene, Eric and Effie.

This paperback edition first published in 2019
by Andersen Press Ltd.
First published in Great Britain
in 2018 by Andersen Press Ltd.,
20 Vauxhall Bridge Road, London SW1V 2SA.
Copyright © Tony Ross, 2018
The right of Tony Ross to be identified
as the author and illustrator of this work
has been asserted by him in accordance
with the Copyright, Designs and Patents Act, 1988.
Printed and bound in China.
All rights reserved.
10 9 8 7 6 5 4 3 2 1
British Library Cataloguing in Publication Data
available.
ISBN 978 1 78344 766 4